Disposable Dagger

Kielen King

Monarkie DCS
915 Broadway Street, Ste 100
Vancouver, WA 98660
monarkie.digital

Table of Contents

Operating on too little sleep, Xavial Dedmon was in no mood to be sent out on a long-term undertaking in extremely deep space. He sat in his Verlox Voll chalet with a successfully negotiated commerce transport contract with Onarai Logistics, an empty credit transfer case, and a few holographic albums of Old Earth musicians he'd been after for at least 10 years. Now, here was Armitage Bek once again requiring Dedmon to handle some business he clearly had no interest in taking care of himself.

The deal with Onarai was a major win for Aileron Dynamics, considering that Onarai predated Aileron and maintained a 250-year-long string of transporting their own refined mining materials, having utilized mercenary teams of borderline illegal fighter/escort craft. The Cohort had been trying for decades to convince the leadership of Onarai to restructure their transportation operation to align with Interstellar Cohort guidelines in order to, first, benefit the Cohort via lucrative transportation deals, and second, further push the remaining mercenary contractors toward insolvency. Mercenary corporations were relatively wealthy, well-armed, and expensive to keep under control. The Interstellar Cohort maintained strong bureaucratic control over nearly all the colonized planets. However, its enforcement capabilities were directly affected by how much commerce was forced through its doors to fund weapon and equipment needs. The Cohort exhorted plenty of financial and legislative force—which worked well for planets that relied on the commerce the Cohort generated. However, despite having generated large amounts of wealth for all member-planets, the Cohort's managing members hoarded the lion-share of the galaxy's riches, leading to a starved budget that made their military and enforcement actions needlessly difficult. This left a hole large enough for various mercenary groups to fly several large fighters through while thumbing their noses at the Cohort. Now, the Cohort was the controlling partner of Onarai thanks to Dedmon.

—

"Dedmon!" Bek launched at Xavial, with a cordial yet authoritative tone, as the vid call opened. "I trust you have taken in my full briefing on the way back."

"Yeah, so…" Dedmon began. "Why am I doing this one again? This sounds like babysitting a bunch of legally questionable misfits on a deep space run. Why aren't the Mertile twins on this kind of thing?"

"You know I cannot trust them with anything confidential," Bek responded. "As soon as they lay eyes on this, every mercenary in Cohort territory will be in our business."

"But this is a deep space expedition. It could be months or even years before mercs had any idea of what this is. Hell, I don't even know what this is about," Xavial added. "C'mon, don't make me do this shit, Arm. I just got back with a stack of new albums and I promised my lady I would take her out to do something nice."

Bek chuckled. "Xavial, please. You have known this poor woman for what, two months? And one of those months was you, off-world, on a job I gave you. What is the name on this one…Cyra ?"

"I haven't told any—" Dedmon started.

"I always know," Bek interrupted with a smirk.

It was clear that his boss and almost-friend was giving him a hard time, but Dedmon didn't like this. He knew Bek always had eyes in every corner of Cohort territory, but as his right hand and often shadow agent, Dedmon usually was the person that set up those eyes. This was first time Armitage Bek let slip that he had eyes on Xavial as well. When you are the person tasked with handling a CEO as powerful as Bek's work, you learn how to keep your mouth shut and avoid paper trails at all costs. Bek having this information was not a good sign under any circumstance and revealed the fact that Dedmon was not as trusted as he once thought.

Compartmentalizing that concern for a later time, Xavial continued his protest, "Still, this sounds a lot like babysitting, and I haven't been that low on the payroll for at least 10…11 years now. Months of travel there and back, cold-ass cryo-sleep, shit food, rock hard bunks, and a hundred-plus people, many of which are near felons that I have to keep in line. I've done nothing but director-level work these last few years. Shit, you don't even make me follow protocol in the office. I don't get it. Did I piss you off or something?"

"Not even in the slightest," Bek reassured. "I am going to level with you. This task is paramount because it stands to be lucrative—extremely lucrative. This is the kind of prize that will snap these mercenary corporations out of existence and retire you and I with the amount of credits we will reap. Granted, there will be some scraps for the remaining worlds, but you and I—we will win more than you can imagine. I need this to be run efficiently. I need it to be run correctly. And I need it to be run quietly. And there is no one I trust to do this more than you. This is not a punishment, Xavial, I assure you. This is very much akin to the Old Earth adage, 'If you want something done right, do it yourself.' Except in this case, you are 'myself.' Or me. Or…you are you being myself for me. Yes, I think I prefer it that way.

"Furthermore," continued Bek. "This is a research vessel—a sizable cruiser intended for long range excursions. For starters, you will be in command on this mission. Sure, there will be security types and scientists all with their own hierarchies and procedural expectations, however, the mission is yours. That means captain's quarters, real food instead of that protein slop they feed the Cohort troops, and as many of your personal effects as you would like to have loaded on board—including your albums. Command. Comfort. Credits. All yours for a job that will not even make the news feeds."

With a heavy sigh, Xavial Dedmon relented and slumped back in his chair having realized his rest and relaxation plans were dashed on the rocks outside his expensive chalet. As much as he hated this, a job that would pay him enough credits to retire would make what he'd already amassed adequate to put his plan for Aileron Dynamics and Armitage Bek in motion.

"When am I leaving?" Xavial inquired.

"I am surprised you are still sitting there," Bek quipped as the call disconnected.

Then it hit him like a load of Pilian ship beams. Armitage Bek just sent him on a last-minute job he knew nothing about—despite being the only person outside of Bek that did any planning. Bek also just let on that he's been watching him in some capacity. It's extremely deep space. Based on the distance specified that briefing, even light beam transmissions would take about 48 hours to arrive. He'd have any comfort from home he wanted to bring along, and after all of that, he still didn't have a mission directive or any idea of why he was really going out there. All he possessed was command of a research vessel, a promise of unrealized credits, and vague briefs about a pilot, some random security officer, a few scientists, and a terrorist from Corinth. This absolutely smelled of a chess piece being quietly removed from the board.

"I'm pretty sure I just got fucked," Dedmon said aloud as he stared at the offline call screen.

[—]

I

The year is 3248. The Interstellar Cohort is a massive and powerful commerce guild that has its hands in nearly every lucrative deal in the Milky Way. Between interfering in local elections, purchasing then shutting down rivals, and exerting military level enforcement of their agendas, the Cohort is one of the most powerful entities in the galaxy with virtually no oversight or restraint. Having been in existence for the better part of 200 years, the Cohort has become so commonplace that no one questions their presence or motives within business and political affairs. The Cohort operates at the behest of its most powerful and wealthy members.

Currently, only one individual meets those criteria: Armitage Bek, CEO of Aileron Dynamics. As for the remaining board members, Bek operates an intricate ruse that assures them that their votes determine the actions the Cohort takes. As its "elected" head, Bek's position comes with a certain level of inherent trust and respect, allowing him to announce the results of voted matters as he sees fit.

Membership in the Cohort does not come easy. Rumors swirl of nefarious ways some have become members, and the amount of wealth required to receive the coveted "Conference Invitation" means that few are willing to ask too many questions of Bek.

Bek's Aileron Dynamics is the largest and wealthiest member of the Interstellar Cohort. It functions as the corporate voice for the Cohort's affairs. The company is the galaxy's largest technology, space flight, and military research conglomerate. The next largest competitor, HoloForm, Inc., is a mere one-fifth as large as Aileron Dynamics. Aileron possesses more capital than three mid-sized planetary governments combined. Their publicly traceable annual earnings are far less than what the organization actually brings in—as evidenced by their intangible presence on many worlds, coupled with the existence of their very own "law enforcement" agency: Interstellar Cohort Law Enforcement (ICLE).

Aileron Dynamics's public communications present the company as a deep space exploration & resource gathering pioneer that excels in the art of developing and launching next generation deep space transports. Unbeknownst to the public, most of the ship design & building is contracted to, and executed by, The Pilian (PEE-lee-an) Shipwright Doyen on Xavial's homeworld of Pili. The Shipwright Doyen is paid handsomely to nod in agreement as Aileron Dynamics uses their innovations—masking them as the lead products from the nearly fictitious 'Deep Space Logistics' brand. Not-so-mysteriously, no matter how many planets boast having Pilian engineered vessels, the Doyen always proudly comes in second to Aileron Dynamics in every annual fiscal report. However, any pilot who's flown enough ships across the Milky Way would recognize a Pilian build with an Aileron nameplate slapped on it, but the average civilian has no knowledge of the back door dealings that prop up a corporation's line of research, development, and physical products.

Aileron and the Cohort are powerful and powerful entities need powerful individuals to run them. Armitage Bek is the pinnacle of powerful individuals, yet even he needs assistance on matters of import from time to time. That assistance comes in the way of his personal fixer: Xavial Dedmon.

—

Xavial Dedmon approached the Onarai cruiser, which was sitting in orbit around Brahmanda in the Lyra system—the planetary center of all Interstellar Cohort commerce and home of the Aileron Dynamics corporate city. He was positive that he was wasting his time, but absolute that he would leave with the deal Aileron Dynamics had been planning.

"Xavial Dedmon on approach at docking speed. Approach vector point four-five, zed nineteen. Aileron Dynamics confirmation   five-zero-zero-delta-three-nine-eight," Dedmon announced over the comm.

"Aileron, five-zero-zero-delta-three-nine-eight, you are cleared for docking. You are assigned bay one-three B," came the response ten seconds later.

Bay thirteen…, Dedmon mused to himself. *Already trying to move the bad luck in my direction.*

Xavial confirmed his assigned landing location and brought his diplomatic corvette into the docking bay of the Onarai cruiser allowing the autopilot to orient and dock the ship in its assigned parking space. Dedmon's diplomatic vessel was dressed the part while masking several shielded weapons installations and a personal arsenal of weapons that effectively made him a one-man incursion force, if necessary. However, this trip was solely for the purpose of securing a transport contract with the notoriously independent Onarai Logistics. Xavial had no plans of bringing weapons to bear during this endeavor, but he never went anywhere unprepared for hostile hosts. Dedmon stood up, checked the appearance of his professional attire, properly hid a few personal protection items and made his way down the two decks to the exit ramp. As Xavial descended the ramp of his ship, he was met by a single valet in the docking bay.

"Greetings, Director Dedmon. I am Valet Orinian and I will be escorting you to the CEO's private conference room for your meeting," Orinian announced with a dry and uninterested tone.

Xavial wasn't a director within Aileron, but he was enjoying the show of respect and let it continue. Giving an approving nod and offering no response to the obviously callous greeting, he followed the valet on to a lift, through a bay entry door. After rising a couple of decks and exiting the lift, the two of them turned down several more corridors, up another lift, and onto the rear of the ship's command deck, opposite the bridge. Upon leaving the lift, Xavial turned to find the valet had remained on the lift and barely remarked before the lift door shut, "Second door on the left. Sit. Wait." Not particularly thrilled with being spoken to like a Pilian grass hound, he kept a stoic face, turned, and made his way to the conference room.

With 25 decks and a length of 180 meters, these cruisers felt more like space stations than moving vessels. The size, however, made it feasible for a corporation like Onarai to have entire divisions of its business in orbit wherever the need arose. Whenever Dedmon found himself a board a corporate cruiser—Aileron or otherwise—he made it a point to enjoy the massive mobile spectacle. The lift rides and his solo walk to the conference room gave Xavial all the time he needed to appreciate his current surroundings before letting himself through the clearly marked conference room entryway and taking a seat while he waited for his hosts.

Forty-five minutes later, a very perturbed Xavial Dedmon was greeted by a tall stocky man wearing an obvious civilian suit retailored to resemble a military uniform. This was the CEO of Onarai Logistics, Zsarian Conoveh. He walked confidently to the opposite side of the long conference table intended to seat no less than 20 attendees. He did not take a seat, however. Instead, he stood menacingly behind the chair across from Dedmon, placing his hands on its back. Conoveh made sure he was cinematically posed in front of the viewport opening which provided an impressive orbital view of the planet below. This was obviously intended to establish dominance in the conversation and potentially intimidate his visitor, but Xavial had experienced far worse in his work under Armitage Bek and outwardly returned the same flat, sterile energy he'd received from the valet that greeted him upon arrival.

"Welcome Mr. Dedmon," offered Conoveh in a sly tone. "I've heard much of your exploits—or at least, those of your CEO."

In a sour mood from the dismissive interactions and needlessly long wait, Xavial reminded himself to stay calm and just get the contract signed. Once that was done, all of this posturing would mean nothing. Besides, it was understandable that Onarai would be less than thrilled with the necessity of this meeting. A series of botched transport jobs coupled with a few stolen shipments, courtesy of their mercenary friends, placed Onarai in a very disadvantageous position. Their already slim margins had been decimated by a perfect storm of lost and stolen shipments, putting them at odds with multiple delivery partners and creditors. As a result, Onarai was on the brink of insolvency. After 250 years of success, they were now faced with finding a sizable influx of credits or suffering the likelihood of their executive hierarchy being hunted and killed. Mercenaries are a formidable tool when the cash is flowing and an instrument of personal destruction when debts are due. Onarai had been dancing on both sides of this line for a century, often entering into deals that required them to compensate their mercenary partners directly from their acquired resources-in-transit. As a result, taking losses from one set of mercenary partners meant lacking the ability to immediately compensate another. And mercenaries have never been known for their compensatory patience.

"I'm curious about that reference to my CEO," Xavial offered. "However, I am here on official Aileron business and would like to get to the heart of the matter rather quickly."

"Ahh. Focus and determination," beamed Conoveh. "Two of my favorite!"

"Excellent," Dedmon began. "Our first order of business is to outline—"

"Here's the thing, Director." Conoveh interrupted. "Before Onarai is free and clear to enter into an agreement with Aileron, there is a matter of concern we will require your services to address."

Already concerned with this redirection, Xavial prompted the CEO to continue with an exaggerated, "Go on…"

"I am positive you are aware of our current status with various mercenary clients and benefactors," Conoveh continued. "Unfortunately, we are in a particular spot of debt with one Singularity Ltd.—hilariously corporate moniker for a pack of mercenaries, I must say. More specifically, we are 'in the red' if you will, to the tune of some 15.4 million credits. Of importance to Aileron is the fact that, as far as mercenaries are concerned, any business partner or associate of the party in debt becomes an equally legitimate target for retribution. Needless to say, we would absolutely abhor putting Aileron in a position to suffer losses on our behalf."

An irritated Dedmon spoke up, "So, pay them and let's get on with our business—"

"Ahh…to that point," Conoveh added. "Due to our current persona non grata status with a number of our creditors, we are in a difficult position as it pertains to rendering that payment. Frankly, I do not wish to have any members of my executive team executed for attempting to deliver said payment—only to have our adversaries claim the payment was never made. That would obviously put us in a position to have to make further payments despite having such a large sum extracted from us while also being subject to additional attacks.

"And before you ask, yes, we have considered having a less crucial member of our staff sent to deliver our obligation. However, would Aileron send a low-level employee out into the dark of space with 20 million of *your* credits with your lives on the line?"

Dedmon smirked at the thought.

"Of course not," Zsarian mused. "Thus, we are subjected to imposing upon you to act as our surrogate. This will provide us with a 3rd party witness to the transaction and subsequently give our debtors no reason to bare teeth to an envoy they have no quarrel with."

Xavial knew this CEO was full of shit, but this level of ignorance could not be accidental. There were zero universes where the CEO of Onarai was unaware that Aileron had been working its political influence to rid the galaxy of mercenary corporations for decades. They were natural enemies and no one with a functioning brain could think otherwise. This left the only other option: Aileron was being manipulated and placed directly in the path between the mercs and Onarai. And Xavial Dedmon knew better than to accept this ruse at face value.

"I will need to confer with my CEO before I'm able to make such a deviation," Dedmon explained.

"Please!" Conoveh encouraged. "Take the time you need. I'll return once you have confirmed your course of action." Zsarian Conoveh then turned sharply and confidently exited the room using the same doorway as before.

Amused and sure how the next conversation would transpire, Xavial pulled the comm out of his pocket, slapped it on his arm, and opened his usual secure link with Armitage Bek. Dedmon knew there was no way he could ensure the walls of the Onarai vessel were not listening. So, he settled for the knowledge that at least no one outside this ship would be privy to the discussion.

"I trust we have a deal, yes?" inquired Bek immediately upon opening the connection.

"Not quite," Xavial responded. He spent the next few minutes detailing the request and direct statements from the Onarai CEO, knowing Bek would refuse such a fool's errand.

"Do it," Bek said flatly.

"What?!" barked Dedmon. "First, *why* would we do this? Second. Why would you send *me* to do this and expect me to walk out of there alive?"

"Please, my friend," Armitage injected calmly. "Meditative breaths if you require them," He added, just shy of a mocking tone. "For starters, I know you to be capable, effective, and nobody's fool. You are always prepared and you have yet to fail in any capacity since entering the Aileron offices. Additionally, I am always prepared for contingencies, and we will suffer no losses on this endeavor. I assure you. Proceed with their request and follow up with me once the contract is finalized."

To the chagrin of Xavial, the comm disconnected abruptly. Clearly aware of the conversation, Conoveh immediately reappeared in the conference room with a smile that was undoubtedly amused at Dedmon's predicament.

"Have you completed your check-in?" Zsarian inquired as he approached the table, placing three credit transfer cases on it.

A visibly perturbed Xavial Dedmon simply stared back at the CEO with a fury burning just below the surface.

"Here is how we will proceed," the CEO began. "We know you have arrived with a credit transfer case containing the 20 million acquisition cost. We have already taken the liberty of retrieving it from your ship."

Immediately, the door slid open behind Dedmon and Valet Orinian entered, walked past a surprised Xavial, and placed the transfer case on the conference table.

Conoveh continued as his valet separated the credits into the three new transfer cases, "As a show of good faith, we will split the payment as follows. The 15.4 million owed to Singularity will be placed in this 1st case here. In this second case, 2.1 million will be placed as your personal compensation for placing yourself in harm's way on our behalf. The remaining 2.5 million will be accepted and noted by Onarai Logistics as received payment pursuant to your acquisition contract."

Not easily distracted, Xavial was unusually irritated at this collection of changed directives and perceived pressure from both sides. Dedmon stood sharply and snatched up the two new credit transfer cases, turned to leave, and barked as he exited the conference room, "I will *not* be going unarmed."

A partial response could be heard as he approached the lift amidst the auto-closing of the conference door, "Of course! The coordinates will be sent to your—"

Fueled by anger, Dedmon found his way back to the hangar and swiftly boarded his corvette, tossed the transfer cases on one of his tables before he made his way up the levels and through the door leading to his two-man bridge. Pulling up the coordinates that were, in fact, already present in his system, Dedmon powered up, received clearance for takeoff, and exited the Onarai cruiser. Once clear, he ramped up his intrastellar drive and pushed off for the edge of the Lyra system.

[—]

II

As far as the Interstellar Cohort was concerned, a system's boundary ended with the furthest planet from the star. As such, Interstellar Cohort legal jurisdiction did not extend to the desolate regions of space just outside the system. This was where mercenary corporations preferred to operate from. Singularity Limited was one of those corporations. Having made use of an old mining space station that was scheduled to descend into its nearby moon's atmosphere for demolition, Singularity utilized several massive freighters and the station's rotational boosters to slowly tow the space station past the Lyra system's boundary over a 3-month period. A space station's unauthorized relocation should have drawn a lot of attention. However, the one constant with all corporate entities was an affinity for profit. A decommissioned station no longer requiring a costly planet-side salvage crew to remove debris? Perfect. The free disposal service simultaneously created a gigantic, free corporate headquarters that Singularity christened: Almalath.

While the trip was not excruciatingly long, it gave Dedmon plenty of time to stew about his predicament while loading and equipping a few of his less-detectable personal protection items. After approximately three hours of flight time, Xavial disengaged the intrastellar drive and began heavy braking to slow himself down on approach to the Singularity headquarters. After allowing the ship to drop to a reasonable approach speed, he dropped all diplomatic pretense and brought his weapons system online. Dedmon knew his vessel would be scanned and the online weapons system coupled with the lack of a targeting ping would present a clear communication of capability without intent. As he arrived, Xavial transmitted his identification and landing code. A moment later, confirmation arrived, and he was given an open bay to set down in.

As Xavial approached the exit ramp, he angrily grabbed the cash prize he was to deliver and made his way out into the station's hangar bay. This time, he was greeted by a crew of five dressed in as perfect a mix of pirate and tactical garb as one could imagine. Dedmon smirked as he thought to himself that this crew of idiots probably had the brute force to steal an antimatter missile off a Cohort carrier, but the sheer ignorance would simultaneously result in them reducing themselves and half a planetary system to carbon dust.

"That's far enough," the individual standing at the head of the pack barked.

Following his internal scoffing at the group of misfits, Xavial reminded himself to stay calm and alert. He was angry as hell earlier, but his one strength has always been the ability to stay measured and relaxed the more intense his circumstances became. The one lesson he learned from Bek early on and never forgot was that his anger was a distraction. Anything that took his mind off what he was there to do was a liability. Liabilities led to losses and Xavial Dedmon was not in the business of taking losses.

Xavial said nothing in response to the group. He held up the transfer case in both hands and waited for the next action. The head of the group took a few steps closer to Dedmon and smirked.

"Xavial…interesting. I didn't think Onarai employed messenger bots," sneered the short, but stocky bearded man with a few key teeth missing. Chuckles poked out of the peanut gallery behind him.

Dedmon stood silent and stoic.

The second of the bunch spoke up, "Aww, this one's no fun. Maybe we should take his ship as part of the payment."

"Five O seven eight." Dedmon replied flatly. "What?" came the reply from the group's leader.

"The fifty seventy-eight model of the Pilian Diplomatic Corvette series comes standard with multiple ownership verification systems. Voice recognition. Fingerprint scans. Retina scans. DNA scans at transfer of ownership, and a little piece of paper that says it's mine stuck to the console in front of the pilot's seat—plus…" Dedmon added matter-of-factly. "A few…after-market modifications including, but not limited to, a cockpit kill-box incinerator, airlock ID-failure flushing system, and a noxious gas A/B switch calibrated for scrubbing or infill as the need arises. Long story short, you take my ship without my verification bypasses, you don't make it out of this docking bay."

"OK, smart-ass," the leader snapped. "Move!"

The remaining four crew members quickly made their way behind Xavial with stun pistols drawn. The leader of the group, having turned slightly, was now pointing at a small lift door at the rear of the docking bay. Satisfied, he had made his point following the mild threat, Dedmon took up a steady pace and made the roughly twenty-meter trek to the lift. The door opened. Xavial wasn't pushed, but the energy and proximity of the crew at his back made it very clear he needed to enter the lift with some level of urgency. He obliged them.

The lift ride lacked any visual markers so Dedmon decided to feel his way, closing his eyes and listening to the station breathe. His internal count suggested he'd descended about three or four levels into the station when the lift came to an abrupt stop. The door slid open, Xavial turned around, and exited into what he immediately recognized as the station's brig. Everyone knew a jail cell when they saw one. For a moment, Xavial allowed the sinking feeling in his stomach to win. He snapped out of it quickly, recalling that he hadn't been searched or even questioned about whether he was armed.

One of the grunts, who appeared to be low man on the roster, rushed passed the short gauntlet of four holding cells to a heavy door at the back of the room and pushed it open, revealing what was clearly an interrogation room.

"Inside. Sit." instructed the lead merc as he took the transfer case out of Dedmon's hands.

Xavial nodded, quickly scanned the space for any exit points, and cautiously made his way into the interrogation room. The room was small and dimly lit with just a blocky metal desk, two chairs, and the recessed lighting in the ceiling. The walls were smooth metallic plates, giving the room a sterile and restrictive feel. The door slammed shut no sooner than he cleared the entrance. He began to regret taking on this assignment even more as he was now a prisoner on a mercenary space station with a vulnerable 17.5 million credits in his possession, an inadequate selection of weapons to fight off an entire squad of mercs, and no visible escape routes.

"Bek better be right about this," he muttered to himself as he looked around for anything that might give him a clue of what was about to happen. He looked again at the walls and saw nothing that would suggest he could make it out of here any other way than through the door he just entered. The desk facing him and the chair behind it looked like ordinary office issued furniture, as they were likely holdovers from the corporate mining operation originally run out of this station. He stood behind a chair that was clearly meant for him as the subject of interrogation. As he stepped around the chair and pulled it up behind him to sit, he noticed a seam in the floor plates. It led away from him, losing itself under the desk in front of him. He twisted to first look behind the chair and then underneath. Xavial soon spotted the connecting seams that formed a rectangular shape around the chair.

"What millennium is this?" Xavial posed under his breath. "There's no way there's a trap door on this station. Who in the hell would—"

The sound of the locking mechanism on the door snapped Dedmon back to the matter at hand. However, just before his hosts entered the room, he readjusted his chair so the two right legs were just outside the right edge of the seam in the floor. He really didn't want to believe something as comical and archaic as a trap door would exist in the brig of a mining space station, but it would be much worse for his ego were he to fall into one.

The lead merc of the crew that led him to the interrogation room entered trying his best to look as though he were in charge—and failing miserably. Xavial Dedmon worked for the most powerful CEO in all of human-colonized space and had seen his share of CEOs, political giants, and other leaders. This false bravado and exaggerated walk of command fooled no one that had ever spent time around individuals with tangible power. The man walked around the table and took the other seat, confidently placing the credit transfer case on the desk between them.

Tiring of all the posturing, Xavial spoke up. "Look, this is entirely too much for a payment delivery. I would prefer to just be on my way. You have what's yours."

"Well, Mr. Dedmon, my associates and I, we believe your payment is a touch light," the merc stated. "You see, 15.4 million is what you brought, however, 20 million is what we're going to require to complete the transaction and clear your benefactors over at Onarai."

Dedmon responded sharply. "First. I've seen the ledger. Onarai owes you 15.4 and that's what I delivered. Anything more between you and Onarai is not my business. Now, I would appreciate it if you'd quit fucking with me and let me get back to work."

The merc became visually irritated and leaned forward on the desk. "You need to watch your goddamned tone when you address me."

Xavial snapped back, "Shut that shit up. You're not even the boss on this boat—got me down here wasting my fucking ti—"

Before he could finish, the panel beneath his chair gave way. However, as a result of the two legs he'd placed just right of the seam, only the left side dropped in. The opening in the floor was only eighteen inches deep. As the chair tilted to the left, Xavial used the momentum to roll out of the chair towards the wall, simultaneously retrieving the tranquilizer pistol secured in his waistband. For a spit second, Dedmon was sure he heard the high pitch electrical whine of a laser powering up, but he saw no weapon in the merc's hand. The merc was, instead, standing behind the desk attempting to draw his stun pistol. But not before Xavial hit him center-mass with two darts from the tranquilizer pistol. The merc looked down to see darts sticking out of his chest, instead of something more damaging, and delivered a smirk in Dedmon's direction. It was mere seconds before the merc's expression shifted to wide-eyed panic. The merc's body seized and he stood frozen for five seconds until blood began to leak from his eyes and nose. The merc then fell to the floor behind the desk, dead.

What the man mistook for a tranquilizer was a nasty concoction with the moniker: Frozen Lava. The effect of this highly illegal, man-made toxin sends the body into a cold shock response while simultaneously dissolving internal tissues at the point of injection. It works especially fast if the point of entry is anywhere near vital organs. The poison is so deadly, the punishment for possession on most Cohort planets is lifetime imprisonment. Dedmon has been able to acquire a steady supply for the last five years, unbeknownst to even Armitage Bek. Because he is often tasked with handling the CEO's affairs clandestinely, the poison is a handy tool that draws little attention until Dedmon is often long gone.

Xavial knew he would have a lot of company soon and he was boxed in. He slid over to the dead merc to check his body for anything that might be useful. He quickly located an access card he figured would allow him to navigate his way off this deep-space trash pile. Next, he snagged the merc's stun pistol, knowing he was going to have to fight his way out of here. He peered up over the desk toward the door that would soon have a team of mercs itching to get through it. That's when he saw it. Along the door was the faint hairline trail of a laser burn. It was exactly at the desktop's height and width. Looking underneath the desktop revealed a recessed button. Completing the obvious next step, Xavial pushed the button and sure enough, he heard the very same electrical whine from earlier and saw a whisp of smoke start on side of the door and quickly travel along a straight path to the other side. Dedmon stopped to wonder just how many unsuspecting victims had their chair dropped into a shallow hole only to immediately experience a high-powered laser run across some portion of their head or neck. He quickly shook the thought as the sound of the merc team arriving at the door commanded his attention.

"This doesn't have to get messy!" Dedmon yelled through the closed metal door, taking cover behind the desk.

"Come on out!" came the reply. "We won't jump you…promise!"

"Look," Xavial offered in response. "You can still get your money! It's all here. I just want passage to my ship and off the station!"

"You took one of ours," a merc called out. "Now it's our turn!"

"Hey!" Xavial barked. "This asshole literally tried to take my head off!"

Immediately the door burst open and a bulky merc in full armor and weapon drawn stormed in to force the action. Dedmon immediately hit the switch under the desk sending the white-hot laser right across the man's mid-section. The mercenary instantly dropped to his knees, screaming in pain as the top half of his body began falling to one side, independent of his lower half. Xavial reached over the desk with his left hand and popped the merc in the neck with a fresh Frozen Lava dart. 10 seconds passed as Dedmon listened and the crew outside the door watched their comrade expire before their eyes. One of the more experienced in the group realized what was happening and screamed out, "Frozen Lava! Fall back! Fall back!"

With their weapons drawn and not taking their eyes off the interrogation room, the mercs slowly withdrew in formation and made their way on to the lift at the other end of the holding cells. Xavial took a look from behind the desk and stood up straight. He adjusted his overcoat and took a seat on the interrogator's side of the desk, weapons laid calmly in front of him.

Sixty seconds passed before a woman's voice broke thought on the station's comm system. "Mr. Dedmon, your reputation precedes you and your abilities are the perfect arrival. I am Mutar Vellakeen. I am what you would refer to as the leader of

Singularity, although our functional structure varies in many ways. As you have proven yourself to be more than capable, I will meet with you. Please stow your weapons and note that the weapon within the desk has been deactivated. I will arrive shortly."

Dedmon, now feeling he was in a position of strength, calmly placed his weapon back in its slim holster and slid the merc's over to his left. He intended to display goodwill, hoping that would aid his exit, but wanted very much to have a visible weapon in play. Two minutes later, the lift opened and a tall slim woman in body armor, and standard issue merc gloves, exited the opening. She made the trek past the holding cells and entered the open door with an unnerving grin on her face.

"Vellakeen, I presume." Xavial stated.

"I am," she responded.

Vellakeen then picked up the lopsided chair in the shallow pit-trap and, as it lifted off the ground, the trap door reset itself. She set the chair back down and took a seat, turning her body to the side and not looking at Dedmon.

"By our code, you retired two of my quality operators. And, as such, the next order of business would be to dismember you, vacuum pack your remains, and return you to your employer. Is there any reason why we should not proceed?" asked Vellakeen.

"Frankly speaking," Xavial began. "I can preserve the lives of you and your entire organization."

Instantly amused, Mutar Vellakeen was unable to hide her facial expression before exclaiming, "I cannot ingest this information fast enough. Please do tell."

Dedmon sat back in his chair and confidently responded, "I am quite done with this endeavor at this point, so I'm not going to dance around it. Inside this transfer case, along with 15.4 million credits, is a very small, but very high-yield anti-matter explosive. I do not appreciate being sent into potentially deadly encounters with information that has been withheld from me. Nor am I thrilled with ending up as collateral damage and being used as a delivery system for a hit I never agreed to perform—despite Aileron's position on mercs."

Dedmon continued, "As such, I am willing to do a number of mutually beneficial things. First, I will disarm this explosive and surrender it to you to do with as you will. Second, your revenge for this attempt will also act as my revenge for being put in this position. I will facilitate putting you in the same room with Zsarian Conoveh, weapons included. Lastly, I will refrain from retiring any more of your operatives as long as no additional retribution is attempted in regard to today's events."

After a moment of contemplation, Vellakeen spoke up, "An opportunity to deliver a personal message to Onarai is difficult to pass up. However, once you've secured your deal, where does that leave us? We were pulling a generous profit from this…arrangement."

Unsure about Singularity's knowledge regarding Aileron's logistics, Dedmon decided to present a bluff to his host. "You are no doubt aware of Aileron's disdain for mercenaries. Here's what I can promise as someone who has the ear of the CEO: In return for your assistance in this matter. Aileron will no longer use its enforcement resources to interfere with Singularity affairs. We make no guarantee regarding other entities or any of your potential associates, however, you will be left to conduct your business as you see fit—save the occasional theatrical engagement, allowing us to keep up appearances and such."

Xavial knew damn well he could not guarantee that Bek would honor such an agreement, nor could he personally sway the chain of command in the I.C. security forces to make this a reality. Instead, Dedmon banked on the hope that Singularity did not possess enough intel to call bullshit on this very attractive offer.

Mutar sat quietly contemplating her next step. Then it came to her, "First, I don't handle first-person encounters. How do you convince me that this will not be a voyage that ends in my death? Neither of us are fools and you were, mere minutes ago, fighting for your life from behind this desk."

Xavial provided additional assurance, "True. However, I will be your accompaniment on the trip back. I will announce your arrival as an envoy sent to formalize the acceptance of payment and the conclusion of your mutual business arrangement." He continued, "Feel free to pack one of your cruisers with a security detail and send it along behind us. I will present you as the envoy, granted you mask up somewhat. And if things go south, your security force can ensure that I don't leave there in one piece. I only ask that you bring no explosives. I want to go home too. If everything goes according to plan, you're free to operate as you see fit in Cohort space—barring any murders or assassinations."

"But you're taking my biggest client," Vellakeen insisted.

"And you don't exist to Cohort enforcement," Dedmon countered.

Having the Cohort finally out of Singularity's affairs, seemingly forever, was too good a deal to pass up. Mutar relented with a stern expression and a dry tone, "Deal."

[—]

|||

Xavial Dedmon's diplomatic corvette pulled out of Almalath station and the entry chime to the cockpit sounded just as he engaged the intrastellar drive. Dedmon released the security lock, opting to let his passenger join him.

[BE-BE-BE-BEEP! BE-BE-BE-BEEP!]

Mutar Vellakeen froze just inside the doorway.

"Aht aht aht," cautioned Dedmon. "You're going to have put the guns back in the guest lounge. I have zero interest in being a victim on my own ship."

Vellakeen chuckled. "Oh c'mon. If I wanted to take you, I would have done that when you were still on my station. Conoveh isn't going to give me more than one shot. And I don't plan on needing any more than that. Besides, he's *really* not going to like this one."

That was the kind of statement Xavial knew he would make if he had a particularly nasty surprise in store for someone. He decided against asking any more questions as he figured the less he knew the better. He tossed a smirk in Mutar's direction. Then, he turned on the ship's music system, picked one of his favorite Old Earth classics and reclined in his chair for a quick three-hour nap.

—

Xavial Dedmon was jarred awake by a backhanded slap on the arm from the seat to his right. Wide-eyed and pushing himself out of his slumping posture, Xavial looked over to see Vellakeen pointing out ahead of the ship.

"We're entering their scan radius," she said flatly.

A moment later, alert chimes began ringing as soon as the ship crossed the invisible boundary into the scan range of the Onarai cruiser still orbiting Brahmanda. Xavial reached up and silenced his intended alarm clock and opened a comm channel to announce his arrival and provide the appropriate codes. A moment later, the approval code came in. But this time, there was no verbal acknowledgment. Dedmon figured they wouldn't be too pleased with him making a return visit. Obviously, the plan was for Singularity to end him while simultaneously cutting the head off of their organization with their explosive Trojan Horse.

After a short, but slow, ride into the docking bay, Xavial once again waited while the auto pilot dropped him right back in bay 13B. Dedmon and his travel companion made sure their weapons were properly hidden and made their way to the exit ramp. Oddly, they were not greeted by the callous valet he encountered on his first trip. There was no one. Feeling uneasy, Xavial visually scanned for anything in the docking bay that might be used as an ambush hiding spot. The two of them made their way across the deck and Dedmon recognized that the lift door on the other end of the docking bay was open and waiting for them.

"I'm pretty sure I don't need to tell a merc to keep their eyes open, but you know," Xavial said quietly.

His companion said nothing, maintaining their role as accompanying valet and walking behind Dedmon, keeping their hooded head bowed low. The two of them made their way through the door and onto the lift without incident. As the door on the lift closed, Xavial let out a quick sigh of initial relief.

"I don't do this quiet shit. If you're coming for me, just get to it," he said to no one in particular.

"Relax," Vellakeen responded.

"Don't tell me to fuckin' relax," Xavial sniped.

Vellakeen retorted in a quiet, but stiff, tone, "You quite literally beat the ass of one of my better units while in an enclosed space, *with traps*—the fuck are you on about?"

"Listen," he started. "These bastards just sent me on a death run they were certain would be done by now. Me walking back on to this ship is the last thing they expected *or* wanted. That means I now have to anticipate the myriad ways they might be planning to reduce me to ash."

Now audibly annoyed with Dedmon, Mutar lamented, "You have *got* to be the most skittish coporat—"

"Look," Xavial snapped. "We have a deal to sort this mess out, but I'm not here to take shit from you. Make sure your VEST is on standby and let's just get this finished."

V.E.S.T. or "VEST" was the common name for Aileron Dynamics's proprietary emergency vacuum-exposure undersuit. The deep-space life preserver was originally labeled: Vacuum Exposure Survival Tech-suit. No one in the real world was ever going to say that, so users simply took to calling them "VESTs." The suits were made from a nano-particle-infused smart material that was breathable and comfortable to wear and possessed the ability to reconfigure and extend itself to provide an air-tight seal around the extremities including the wearers head, while rendering a portion of the face covering translucent for visibility. The suits quickly caught on and became a main-stay for asteroid miners and deep-space cargo runners who were all-to-likely to have a catastrophic event while in deep space and ultimately too far away from any reasonable rescue team. Upon introduction, deep-space workers saw a 400% increased survival rate during sudden depressurization events (SDE), revolutionizing safety efforts. The suits quickly found an expanded market among space-faring civilians, solidifying the wearable innovation as the only choice for anyone planning to leave atmosphere.

The lift arrived at the upper deck of the Onarai cruiser. Xavial and Mutar cautiously stepped out, saw no one, and made their way to the conference room, which was strangely missing its conference table. The room was dark and disturbingly silent. Upon entering the room, the door behind them suddenly slid shut and locked with the telltale metallic clank of an emergency lock reserved for SDEs, trapping them inside. The two of them immediately reached for and drew their weapons, ready to open fire. A full minute passed before they could hear the unmistakable sound of something with claws and more than two legs tapping on the metal floor outside the far entrance to the conference room. Breaking the silence was a chilling multi-throated screech piercing the air and sending shivers down their spines.

"Shit. Oxyl hounds," Xavial whispered sharply.

"What the hell is an Oxyl hound?" Mutar queried.

"Very fast. Very angry. Very hungry pack hunters," Dedmon answered.

"You've seen these things before?" Vellakeen inquired.

"Once, in a forest on Corinth. Think dog from Old Earth, nearly twice as tall, fur on the bottom half, rock-hard scales on their top half with blades protruding from the spine—sharp enough to gut you," Xavial explained.

"Shit. Oxyl hounds, indeed," Mutar offered. "What's the plan?"

"No guarantee this will work," Dedmon began. "But stay low and do not look them in the eye. When in doubt, duck or hit the deck.

They often hunt by jumping and using the spines to gut taller animals. With smaller animals, they'll work to slice their bodies and start the bleed so the smell of blood attracts more of the pack to help. Also, their jaws have been rated in comparison to hydraulic presses. You don't want to be bitten. If we're lucky, their instincts will have them trying to cut us open to draw others and that will buy us some time, but I can't imagine Onarai would keep an entire pack onboard—that's like 50 of those damned things."

"What in the hell were you doing on Corinth to find all *that* out?" Mutar prodded.

Dedmon responded, "That's my business, but I will tell you we received a briefing before heading into that forest and nothing will wake you up faster than watching a guy lose a leg trying to dive over a charging group of those demons."

On the other end of the conference room where Conoveh once entered, the door clicked and audibly slid open, revealing the first of four menacing hounds making its way into the conference room. The eyes, bright orange with fury, appeared illuminated in the dim room. Xavial and Mutar braced themselves for the impending fight, having no choice but to stand their ground.

As the hounds made their way into the room, the door slid shut behind them and the sound of the decompression lock engaging was as audible as the snarls emanating from the beasts. The hounds began to display their hunting prowess almost immediately. The first two set themselves at opposing angles around Xavial and the remaining pair followed suit with Mutar. Xavial dropped to one knee, leaning forward, having re-holstered his pair of stun pistols in favor of a curved dagger in each hand. He'd learned enough in his time on Corinth to know that stun pistols were nothing more than a tickle to Oxyl hounds. And in most cases, it only served to piss them off. Vellakeen set her tall frame into a slightly lowered wide stance prepping herself to move left or right as quickly as possible. Having caught a glimpse of Dedmon's weapon swap, she asked no questions and replaced her own stun pistol with a small ballistic pistol. She figured there wouldn't be a more apt time to risk putting a hole in a hull plate.

With frightening speed, the first pair of hounds sprang into action. Each of them angling their spinal blades in mid-air towards Dedmon to create a gauntlet aimed at making fresh cuts in his flesh. He dropped himself onto his back to avoid the lunging pair, bringing is arms out and up to slice at the beasts passing over him. His left hand managed to catch the corresponding hound fur-side, but not deep enough to hit any major organs. His right hand snapped back towards the floor as the missed strike made contact with one of the hardened scales on the beast, sending the energy of the blow back down Xavial's arm. The wounded hound let out a wild sound that resembled a blend of an Old Earth dog's howl and the piercing screech of a massive, wounded bird. The cry was off-putting, but reassuring the damage had been done. The hounds landed on opposite sides from where they began—the wounded one landing awkwardly and dripping blood from the fresh wound. Yet both hounds maintained their intimidating posture.

Shortly after the first pair lunged at Dedmon, the 2nd pair launched a similar attack at Vellakeen. As the two hounds converged on her in the air, she launched herself to the left and fired a shot towards the pair. Twin cries of pain erupted as the projectile passed through the leg of one hound and buried itself in the second hound's mid-section.

"Was that a fuckin' ballistic?!" Dedmon barked from across the room. "You tryin' to kill us?!"

"I'm trying to kill them! You got any better weapons?!" Mutar snapped in response.

Silence came back from Xavial as he stood, looked across the room, and saw one of the hounds stumble toward one of the conference room walls, attempt to pull itself up from the ground, then collapse dead. Turning back to his two adversaries a moment too late, one of the hounds managed to throw itself into Dedmon's right leg, opening a large gash along his outer thigh. Xavial yelled out in pain and dropped back down to one knee, turning his attention back to his pair of attackers just as the second hound lunged for his face. Wide-eyed and reacting quickly, Xavial placed his left forearm under the hound's lower jaw, pushing the beast up and over the top of him. He immediately followed that move by thrusting the blade in his other hand into the creature's neck. The animal completed its in-air arc, landing behind Dedmon with a thud and an expiring exhale.

Now injured and having lost its hunting accomplice, the hound engaged with Mutar was feeling the severity of the wound in its hind leg and was backing up towards the door it entered from, maintaining a defensive snarl and baring its teeth. Recognizing the situation and having no desire to invoke the wounded animal cliché, Vellakeen followed suit and slowly backed away from the hound, bringing her back-to-back with Xavial. Startled by the contact and fearing the remaining hound had come for him, Dedmon whipped around with his knife at the ready.

"Damnit Vella—"

Before Xavial could get her name out of his mouth, Mutar swung her left arm up to the left side of Xavial's head, violently shoving his head out of the way. In the same motion, she brought her right arm up directly in the path of the Oxyl hound that leapt into action while Dedmon was distracted and fired right into the mouth of oncoming creature. The animal went limp while still airborne, dropped to the deck, and slid right up next to its deceased counterpart.

"You're welcome." Vellakeen offered with a smirk. She then reached down and began an entry in the comm on her left arm.

"What the hell are you doing?" Dedmon demanded to know.

"Marking the date and time I got to do the 'you're welcome' bit...been on my list for years," replied Mutar.

Xavial shook his head in comedic disgust just as his own comm started beeping frantically. Both Dedmon and Vellakeen's VESTs activated without warning, sealing their extremities and covering their heads. Once Xavial realized what happened, he pulled his arm up to eye level to check the notification on the comm.

[IMMEDIATE DANGER: HIGH LEVEL AIRBORNE TOXIN. PRIMARY AGENT: STRYCHNINE]

Where the fuck did they get Old Earth poison? Xavial pondered. "Mutar! We got a problem!"

"What now?!" Vellakeen replied over the comm link.

The moment she finished her query, the remaining hound fell onto its side, convulsing violently.

"We gotta get out *now*!" Dedmon responded. "We've got about sixty seconds of filtration in these things and we're dead! You have any rounds left in that thing?" He inquired, pointing at the ballistic pistol she was still holding.

Vellakeen took a brief look at her weapon's readout. "Yeah, five rounds. Armor piercing."

"Holy shit—aahhh whatever. Shoot the viewport!" Xavial commanded.

Confused, Vellakeen protested, "What?! Why? I know I shouldn't have brought it, bu—"

"Do it! *Now!*" Dedmon shouted.

Mutar hesitantly pointed the weapon at the 3-meter-wide stretch of transparent aluminum plating and fired a single shot. The projectile lodged itself in the plate creating a small divot barely affecting its integrity.

"Again!" Dedmon said urgently.

Mutar knew a life and death situation when she saw one and, considering they were in hostile territory, she felt it best not to waste time asking for details. *Survive first, get the particulars later,* she thought. Vellakeen engaged the target lock on the pistol. This set the weapon to lock onto the position of the previously fired projectile, a necessity in this moment. She fired a second shot. This one struck the end of the previous round, creating a noticeable indentation in the surface of the plate.

"Keep firing! We need outta here *ASAP!*" Dedmon insisted. He took a quick look at his comm and the filtration countdown on the VEST was down to 33 seconds.

"Mutar took aim again and voiced into the ether, "Third time wins."

She fired again, striking the previous two shots, sending all three deeper into the plate. However, it was still intact. At that moment, a hull integrity warning began blaring over the ship's internal comm system.

Only two options now, Xavial thought. *Either the crew rushes in to stop what we're doing or we vent to space.* Dedmon landed on the expectation that they weren't coming. That would mean either scrubbing the gas intended to kill them or having to contend with it themselves—a task he was sure Onarai wouldn't be able to convince grunts to endure.

Irritated that the third shot hadn't done the trick, Vellakeen intended to make both of her final two shots count. She lifted the pistol, locked on to the three embedded rounds and fired once more. The next sound the two of them heard was exactly what they were hoping for. The fourth projectile struck the other three, opening up a fist-sized hole in the plate. The breech was immediately followed by the hiss of the room's atmosphere forcing itself into the vacuum of space and the blaring alarms of the ship's decompression warning system. The difference in pressure resulted in the plate briefly bending outward then quickly snapping free of the hull and tumbling out into the void, along with the remaining oxygen, poison gas, Oxyl hound corpses, Mutar Vellakeen, and Xavial Dedmon.

Now 10 meters outside the cruiser, Xavial considered making their way back into the conference room, working out a way to get back into the hangar and retrieve his ship. That plan was quickly extinguished when he noticed the conference room door to the corridor approaching the lift slid open and a six-pack of zero-G suited security troops entered with rifles aimed at the pair.

"Incoming!" Vellakeen warned as the muzzle flashes from all six ballistic rifles sent bullets racing toward the pair.

"Forward!" Dedmon prompted. "Get to the hull! They can't hit us from in there and we can force them to come looking for us in the dark. We can save our oxygen and push around to the bay door."

The VEST was designed as an emergency apparatus, only to be used in life threatening situations. As such, they did not employ any kind of standard propulsion system to facilitate mobility while in vacuum. Instead, the suit made use of the limited oxygen supply to allow for short-burst gas releases to give the wearer the ability to push themselves in a given direction. A user would not be capable of traveling between distant points, but could push themselves toward a rescue vehicle, for example.

Xavial knew the mathematics of a group of men firing at two targets floating in the darkness, 10 meters away, whilst aboard a vessel moving anywhere from 8 to 10 kilometers per second meant there was very little chance Xavial and Mutar would be hit by any incoming gunfire. As the two reached the hull 30 seconds later, they used the lack of light as camouflage and began pulling themselves along the hull of the Onarai cruiser inch by inch. As they made their way towards the docking bay, Dedmon tapped the comm on his arm to activate the rescue protocol on his corvette. He briefly considered that the Onarai forces could have already destroyed his ship, then reminded himself there's no point in worrying about what might have happened and gave the ship time to power up and respond as they pushed forward.

One minute later, the ship responded:

[DOCKING BAY DOORS: ACTIVE AND CLOSING. EXIT DETERRED.]

Xavial responded by instructing the corvette to fire two torpedoes at the bay doors. The response from the ship came back almost immediately:

[AUTHORIZATION FOR INTERNAL ENVIRONMENT BALLISTIC DEPLOYMENT REQUIRED. DAMAGE TO THIS CRAFT, SURROUNDING LIFE FORMS, OR ENVIRONMENT MAY OCCUR.]

Dedmon sent his authorization code giving no consideration to the warning. Once sent, Xavial continued pulling himself along the outer shell of the cruiser with Mutar not far behind. Ten seconds later, the two of them spotted a bright flash at the far end of the Onarai vessel.

"With any luck," Dedmon began. "That's our ride."

"Did you blow a hole in their docking bay?!" an amused Vellakeen inquired.

"I can neither confirm nor deny," Xavial shot back.

"I knew there was something I liked about you!" Mutar chuckled.

Thirty seconds passed before the corvette sped toward the two spacewalkers, smoothly spun around, and opened up an airlock hatch on the underside of the ship. The two of them reoriented themselves and used their boots to kick off of the Onarai hull, launching themselves into the safety of Xavial Dedmon's diplomatic corvette.

As the two made their way into the lower deck of the ship, with the airlock closed and sealed behind them, their VESTs beeped and with a few short mechanical clicks reset themselves to their unused positions. Xavial's comm flashed red with a notification of the structural repairs needed for his Vest to return to optimum functionality. Nevertheless, the suit had performed admirably, reconfiguring itself to compensate for the physical damage caused by the Oxyl hounds prior to providing an air-tight seal.

Dedmon quickly entered a command on his comm to grant Mutar bridge access before stopping below deck to grab some cut paste and a spray applicator to clean up and seal his leg wound.

"I got a contact—bigger than an escape pod—pulling out of the bay at high speed," Vellakeen called out over the ship's comms a moment later.

"Just above that display. Blue switch," Dedmon instructed.

"Nice…says that vessel is coded to Conoveh…jackass was there the whole time?" Mutar posed.

At that moment, the bridge entry door slid open and Xavial entered looking determined and dropped down into the pilot's seat and flipped 3 switches above the flight controls.

[TARGET LOCKED. TRAJECTORY ANALYSIS COMPLETE. PRESUMED DESTINATION: BRAHMANDA — AILERON CORPORATE CITY CENTER]

"Why would this idiot run from his own cruiser?" Mutar asked.

"Think about it," Dedmon suggested. "You sent the liaison of your corporate buyer to what you perceived was his death; only to have him return with your rival. Then you watch them dispose of a pack of wild animals, vent your conference room, crawl along your hull, then blow an actual hole in the docking bay of your company cruiser. Would you hang around to hear them lodge a formal complaint?"

Vellakeen burst out laughing and Xavial could only follow suit.

"We'll head to Aileron Corporate Headquarters. There's a pad at the top of the business center so we can avoid the public space port," Dedmon noted.

"Wow! You get the corporate parking spot? You are pretty high up," Mutar said half-mocking.

"Please," came the slightly annoyed reply.

Thirty minutes later, as the pair set down on the corporate landing pad atop the Aileron Dynamics Business Center, Xavial gave Mutar a quick warning.

"In about 30 seconds, I'm going to get a comm from Bek. Just...don't say anything. He's probably watching us from somewhere nearby, and he will assume there's a situation that needs to be solved by his hand. I would like to avoid that. I'd hate to have to merc—no pun intended—a member of his personal security team. But I will if I have to. And I hired most of those guys," he explained.

"Damn, that's icy," Vellakeen said.

"Listen, those guys are 'shoot first, ask questions never.' It's like trying to command a giant pack of sentient hammers," Xavial added.

[BE-BEEP…BE-BEEP]

Xavial released a labored sigh and slapped the comm on his arm, "Dedmon."

"My friend!" Bek called out sounding genuinely excited. "I see you've made landfall by way of the Business Center. I trust we have a signed acquisition deal in place, yes?"

Dedmon responded, "I'm currently ironing out some final details. I'll update you as soon the deal is complete."

Bek's tone turned inquisitive, "I was not aware that the closing of this deal required a stop on Brahmanda. Is there anything that requires my attent—"

"Look man," Xavial said bringing an abrupt end to his code switching. "You know I get shit done. Let me work. I'll check in."

As soon as the last word left his lips, Dedmon disconnected the comm.

"Did you…just hang up on your boss?" Vellakeen asked in shock.

"He's gonna be pissed, but he'll shut right up once I drop that signed contract in his inbox," Xavial answered. "Besides, we're losing time we could be spending finding Zsarian's coward ass. Let's go."

The two had collected their gear, made their way off the corvette, and completed their walk from the closing hatch of Dedmon's corvette. They waited for the landing pad's lift to arrive from the lower levels, stepped inside, and descended 78 floors to the ground level of the Aileron Dynamics Business Center.

[—]

IV

Xavial Dedmon exited the Business Center street-level lobby with Mutar Vellakeen right behind him carrying a pack housing their weapons, some additional clothing, and one of the credit transfer cases—containing the rewired explosive originally aimed at Vellakeen. Dedmon was focused on his comm. During the long lift right down to the main floor, Mutar clued Xavial in on the method her mercs used to track transfer cases originating from the same location.

Xavial smirked, "Damn, I'm gonna have to file that away for future use." Leaning over to show Mutar his comm, he continued, "See this building here? That's the city commerce guild. It's basically a maze of conference rooms, offices, and commodity vaults. I'm 100% positive Conoveh will be hiding in there—and probably calling in a few favors."

"You think we can use building security to help flush him out?" Vellakeen asked. "This is basically Aileron's planet, right?"

"Yeah, but fuck that," Dedmon retorted. "I wanna handle this myself. He's going to *wish* we had gotten Cohort security involved."

Xavial switched screens on his comm with a quick swipe and called for an Aileron corporate transport, then immediately canceled it.

"Shit. I don't want this in Aileron's records. It's bad enough Bek knows I'm on-world, unscheduled," he added.

He followed up by sending a ping from his personal comm to one of the transit markers on a post outside of the Business Center. Within twenty seconds, one of the local public personal transports pulled up beside them and the pair hopped in.

—

The transport pulled into the parking area underneath the commerce guild tower. Dedmon instructed the driver to drop them off at the discreet corporate entrance towards the rear of the building. This entrance was mainly used by CEOs and government officials looking to avoid the press or, more importantly, competitors looking to glean information on potential deals or allegiances being formed. It was also notoriously free of security feeds for those looking to keep their presence unofficial. Aileron only allowed those at the highest level of the corporate structure to have the necessary digital access badges designated for this entrance.

As the two entered the building, the concierge snapped to attention, dropping her personal comm on the desk and standing to greet the visitors.

"Uh…Welcome, Mr. Dedmon!" the woman said nervously.

"Ms. Oslet," he replied.

A look of confusion replaced her nervous facial expression as she stood there motionless. The two passed her and continued towards the elevator on the opposite side of the lobby.

As the elevator door closed, Vellakeen turned to Dedmon, "I saw that look."

Xavial smirked, "She doesn't know me, personally. But I approve anyone that gets hired for any discreet level position. I weed out the people with backgrounds they're trying to hide or people that just talk too much. I make sure Aileron is leak-proof."

"Hmm…the man with all the info is…dangerous. I like it," Mutar replied, slightly amused.

"Just FYI…I don't date mercs," he added.

"Please," Vellakeen retorted. "You couldn't handle it if I handed it."

Dedmon was bested into silence and said nothing else on the elevator ride to the 15th floor.

The elevator stopped at the 15th floor of the commerce guild complex, the door opened, and the two of them slowly exited the elevator. Instantly, a spray of metal shards embedded themselves into the wall to Dedmon's left.

"Shit! Get behind the wall!" he shouted as he dove into the corridor to his immediate left.

No stranger to live fire, Vellakeen wasted no time attaching herself to the wall plate of the corridor on the right.

"What. The hell. Was that?!" she demanded.

"Sprayer," Dedmon offered, nearly inaudible.

"What?!" prodded Vellakeen as a new batch of metal pieces shot past her hiding spot and lodged themselves into the wall across from her.

"What the hell is a 'Sprayer?'" Mutar demanded.

Dedmon sighed. "So…about five years ago, we needed a way to dispose of millions of tonnes of scrap metal that was filling up planet-side junk depots and orbital trash lanes—"

"Short version, goddamnit!" Mutar barked.

"Basically, we created a fleet of automated sentries capable of utilizing any form of scrap metal as projectiles and deployed them to high profile accounts and A.D. positions. Saved us billions on ammunition and weapons systems," he admitted.

"Why…in the *ab-so-lute* fu—You know what? I don't even care. How do we handle them?!" Vellakeen asked loudly over the salvos that sounded like 100 boots stomping on a steel plate.

"Gimme a minute! I've never had to fight them!" Xavial shouted.

As he pulled up his comm to begin scouring the Aileron network to find any nearby command post or communications tower that might be relaying instructions to the four sentries, swarms of angry shrapnel continued to batter the corner that made up his hiding space. The continued barrages were tearing chunks out of the wall's surface and concrete base material. At this rate, there wasn't going to be a wall to hide behind in a few minutes.

"There's a security comm array on this floor!" Dedmon called out over the barrage of metal shards. "About 40 meters down this corridor. If we can get to it, I can shut these things down!"

"And how exactly do we get there without these things turning us into chopped Gorlo meat?!" Mutar shot back.

Dedmon recalled the stun pistols they brought were in the pack Vellakeen had been carrying. "Cover me with the stunners! When I go, fire at the sentries. They'll redirect their attention."

"Hold on. Why am I bait for the meat grind—" Vellakeen began.

"*NOW!*" Xavial shouted as he pushed himself off the wall and headed down the corridor in a low sprint.

Mutar leaned out from her cover and opened fire with both pistols, sending bright bolts of energy toward the automated defense units. As predicted, the sentries immediately shifted their focus to counter the current threat, giving Dedmon the opening he needed. He made it halfway down the corridor before diving into an open office doorway just as a spray of shrapnel tore through the space he'd occupied a moment before. He made for the door on the other side of the room. This led to an auxiliary security room which acted as backup uniform and small arms storage. It also housed a recessed wall console which allowed for direct monitoring and control of nearby security systems by senior duty guards. If nothing else, the guards followed protocol because right next to the console hanging on the wall was the personal comm patch cable. The patch cable was crucial as it allowed for transmission of access credentials and direct control of the attached systems. Dedmon quickly snagged the cable by its connector and popped it into his comm.

"Twenty more seconds!" he called out. "Almost got 'em!"

"I'm almost out of charge!" Vellakeen warned.

Xavial pulled up his comm and frantically worked to access the local network. If he could just tap into—

"Got it!" he exclaimed.

A moment later, two of the sentries went silent.

"Clear!" Dedmon called out, thinking he had removed the danger.

Mutar emerged from her cover position and quickly dove back into hiding.

Followed by a thunderous wave of loose metal, Vellakeen shouted, "Shit! They're still out there, you ass!"

Confused, Xavial stuck his head out of the doorway only to yank himself back behind the wall before a fresh swarm of jagged shrapnel hit the wall where his face had just been.

"Damnit!" he shouted.

Angrily, Vellakeen started, "Next time you call clear and it's not, I'll fu—"

"I know!" he responded. "They must be on a different command shard. I got 'em in 3…2…"

Just then a loud hiss filled the corridor, followed by the sound of mechanical struggle. Seconds later two incredibly loud thuds shook the corridor like a mini earthquake.

"Clear!" Mutar called out before Dedmon could peek his head out from cover. "What the hell did you do?!"

"I egged them," Xavial smirked.

"You what?"

"I activated the fire suppression system our R&D team cooked up about a year ago. It hits any active burn with a nano-capsule…fills interior spaces of the object with suppressant…encases the whole thing. Looks like an egg," he explained.

Vellakeen shot him a look that all but screamed how ridiculous an invention this was. Dedmon pretended not to notice, straightened his clothing, and the two of them turned only to find themselves staring at Zsarian Conoveh standing at the far end of the corridor, flanked by four armed security officers.

"Impressive," Conoveh sneered. "I figured I'd be out here with forks picking up spare meat."

"Man, listen…" Dedmon replied, keeping his voice steady. "You had the deal—if you even intended to keep it. But now…"

Zsarian chuckled, "I mean… I *could* humor you, but I'm not going to."

Hearing the snap from Conoveh's fingers, the security detail rushed the pair. Xavial managed to duck and kick out the leg of the overly muscular brute to his left, but not before catching a gloved right hand to the left side of his face. The ringing in his ears and the stars his vision were the only sensations he could make out as he tried, in vain, to pull himself to his feet. As the world around him slowly came back into focus, he noticed 3 bulky guards standing around him with a fourth asleep on the ground having caught the corner of a planter on the way down. The other thing he noticed was the absence of Mutar Vellakeen. He fully expected to find her punching a random guard in the face or, at the very least, iterating threats on precisely what she planned to do to Conoveh once this was over."

A little one on one time," Zsarian mused. "Looks like your backup backed the fuck up." Conoveh let out a huge bellowing laugh, amused at his own humor.

The one guard that was conscious and not holding him up by his arms delivered another bell-ringing punch to Xavial's jaw. The blow didn't break his jaw, but it was hard enough to send pain radiating down his neck and into his shoulder. At this point, Dedmon was equal parts in pain and pissed off. The two remaining guards dragged him into a meeting room off the corridor they were currently in.

Dedmon was roughly tossed into a chair just inside the meeting room. He struggled to pull himself upright from his initial pain-induced lurch. He shifted his eyes upward toward the table that was just out of reach and made eye contact with Zsarian Conoveh smirking as he stood on the other side of the room backlit by the large corporate picture window.

"I know this must all be a little frustrating," Conoveh began. "But seriously, did you really think I would allow your corp to take what my forebears spent centuries building with an anti-climactic purchase contract? I would torch you and every last company in the Milky Way before I surrender my family's legacy—and credits."

"Always the money with you people," Dedmon spit out defiantly. "No one has any appreciation for the art of business—of life."

"The *hell* are you on about?" Zsarian prodded. "Nothing gets done in this galaxy without the funds or just plain power. You, of all people, should know better—what, with you working for that snake Bek."

"For someone who hasn't done a fraction for me what Bek has, I'm gonna need you to watch your mouth," Xavial warned.

"Have you seen your predicament?" Conoveh asked, gesturing vaguely around the room. "Threats from you are ringing pretty hollow right now. I'll tell you what. I'll take your—I mean—my money, my company, and our legacy while you reiterate your 'warning' while taking the free route to the ground floor."

The immediate sting of pain and sparkling vision, the result of a gloved punch from one of Zsarian's tough guys, left Dedmon dazed and fighting to regain his senses. Through the ringing in his ears, Dedmon could hear Conoveh's bellowing laugh as he stood watching. Another blow struck Xavial near his left temple and he was on the brink of losing consciousness, nodding through the pain and hazy vision. Between oscillating bits of bright blurred light and total darkness, the strobing view of Zsarian was the last thing visible before Dedmon slipped into darkness.

"—ake up!…Wake up, damnit!"

The sting of another blow radiated across Xavial's face as his cognitive operating system completed its reboot. Feeling anger well up, he noticed this blow was different. It was sharp, yet not as forceful. He blinked a few times to make sure he could focus as he looked up to see Mutar Vellakeen standing in front of him with half of a meeting room apparently snapped out of existence. Dedmon's senses normalized and he was now fully awake trying to ascertain why she was standing there, apparently slapping him awake.

"What the f—,"

"No time," Mutar interjected. " Get up before we lose him."

"Lose him?" Dedmon prodded as he slowly stood up. "What the hell happened to the rest of the room?!"

"Gave him his bomb back," she smirked. "Rewired it to work just like a mining charge; explosive force sent directly into the structure…no external explosion…shook the wall right of the building. He's over there."

Vellakeen pointed to the open space that used to be the windowed wall of the meeting room. Xavial took a few measured steps toward the broken edge of the floor 15 stories up, spotting the fingertips of one Zsarian Conoveh hanging on for his life.

"Damn, Z!" Dedmon called with an amused tone. "I mean, I didn't know where she went, but you had *no one* look for her?"

"Gloat if you want but pull me up!" Conoveh pleaded.

"Looks like you have a decision to make," Vellakeen posited.

Zsarian only let out a grunt as he struggled to maintain his grip on the jagged concrete and exposed rebar.

"She said it," Xavial concurred. "We've all wasted a considerable amount of each other's time with all this bullshit. I, for one, would like to finish this up and get home to a few new albums I've been wanting to listen to. So how about we just get this contract signed, get everyone what they're owed, and everyone can be on their way?"

"Fine! Just pull me up!" Conoveh demanded.

"Nah man, I'mma need you to sign this shit first," Dedmon said flatly.

"I'm hanging off the side of a goddamned building!" came the response.

"Funny that," Xavial began. "I just happen to have a Bio-Signer right here." He kneeled down before continuing," How about I get you to loosen up one of those thumbs and soon as we're signed, we'll go ahead and get you back up here. Hell, maybe we can all grab a drink to celebrate a fight well fought."

Feeling his grasp weakening, Conoveh offered a desperate, "OK! OK! Do it!"

Dedmon reached down and pried Zsarian's left thumb away from the protruding rod it was attached to and slid the Bio-Signer pad right under the digit. A soft chime was heard and Xavial stood up at the edge of the broken room and began tapping away at the comm on his left arm.

"Alllllright, my man! You have been compensated, the deed of sale is complete, the ownership credentials have been transitioned, and Aileron Dynamics is the new controlling partner of Onarai Logistics."

"Fine! Pull me up for fuck's sake!" Conoveh pleaded.

"A word please?" Vellakeen asked, tapping Dedmon on the shoulder.

"What is it?" he asked.

Gesturing him to take a few steps out of earshot of Conoveh, "So…can I vote for just letting him go?"

Xavial interrupted, "What? Free? Now why would—"

"No, stupid," Mutar spit out in a muted tone. "I mean letting him take the 'air-scalator' to the ground floor. He *did* try to off us both."

"Well, *you* tried to off us both at some point to be fair," Dedmon reminded her.

"Yeah, but you promised me I'd get my shot at him. And this is it."

Xavial protested, "Yeah, but c'mon, that ain't right. If you tell a man you're going—"

"Fine," Vellakeen relented.

"Seriously," he continued. "If we pull him up and you wanna have a go at him. I can't stop you, but I want to keep my word at least. Just pull him up for now."

Mutar raised a hand to signal her acquiescence and stepped over to the ledge, "Um…"

Still looking through documents on his comm, Demon added, "Oh yeah, I guess I should give you a hand. He's a big boy."

"Yeah, no…he's…he's outta here," she stated hesitantly.

"I know," Dedmon started. "As soon as we get him up, you can—"

"No. I mean, he's gone," she added.

"Wait, what?" Xavial took his eyes off his comm and stepped over to the ledge. "We just gotta—Where the hell did he go?!"

"I guess he couldn't hold on," Mutar forced through a smirk.

"But—goddamnit, let's…let's just get out of here," Dedmon exhaled.

He took another look at his comm, navigated through a few screens, and noticed a lift on the way up and an auxiliary transport green-lit for a rooftop landing.

"Stairs it is!" he announced, moving briskly out of the meeting room and down the hall opposite the lift they arrived in. Reaching the end of the corridor, the two of them smoothly slipped through the staircase door and began their downward descent as Xavial tapped a few options on his comm and engaged a security lock on every staircase entry door between them and the ground floor. Grinning slightly, Dedmon checked the security feeds from his comm and watched as Conoveh's backup security team rushed into the corridor and went from door to door, finding no one.

He removed the security locks from the staircase doors just as the pair exited on the lower level where they entered. Scared into shape and determined not to be caught off-guard again, coupled with the influx of security personnel rushing into the building just a moment prior, concierge Oslet was on her feet at full attention.

"Everything alright, Mr. Dedmon? …Sounded like there was an explosion." Ms. Oslet inquired.

"Yes, Ms. Oslet. Everything is under control. The security teams will no doubt have everything normalized shortly. As per usual, your discretion is your value."

"Of course, Mr. Dedmon," came the reply. "Enjoy your evening."

Calmly exiting the lower lobby, Xavial signaled for a new public transport, waited about 60 seconds, then the two climbed into their new ride, and exited the parking area unnoticed.

—

As the two exited their transport, Dedmon turned toward the front entrance of the A.D. Business Center.

"No blame assessment here, but there's probably going to be a lot of noise about a hole being blown out of the 15th floor of the commerce guild and Conoveh being found in the debris. Where do you want me to drop you, I assume Almalath will be on someone's radar," Dedmon stated.

"I'm good," Vellakeen replied in a satisfied tone as she began walking in the opposite direction from the entrance.

Dedmon threw out a confused, "Wait, what?! Where are you going?"

"I've got a ride off this rock. Besides…best we split up and not be seen leaving together anyway. Conoveh's biggest business rivals are hardly a secret around these parts," Mutar added. "You forget, I got 15 million waiting for me. I have more than enough to stay out of sight for a while *and* keep my guys paid."

"OK. But you don't want to verify me wiping your data?" he asked in a sly tone, suggesting something more than just checking files.

"Nah, you got it!" Vellakeen shouted back, not breaking stride as she climbed into a transport she hailed while they were speaking. And in true mercenary fashion, Xavial's accomplice vanished into traffic. He stood at the entrance, silent—confused by the abruptness, but not surprised by the outcome.

Letting it roll off is back, Dedmon double-checked the digital signing of the acquisition contract and confidently made his way inside the building, up 78 floors on the lift, and into his corvette to head to his chalet on Pili—satisfying Armitage Bek along the way. Xavial entered the destination coordinates for his trip, fired off the signed contract for Bek's office administrator, and cracked open a new message from Bek before sleeping most of the 12-hour jump to Pili.

—

Dedmon pulled himself up and out of his bunk as his corvette approached Pili. He was just about to enter the atmosphere when he mapped the route to his chalet and set the auto pilot to set down on his private landing pad. Snagging a cup of coffee from his small food space, Xavial caught a glimpse of himself as he passed a mirror. He stopped to take a look at his appearance and saw himself looking a little rough around the edges, but he felt great. The confidence lifted his chest slightly and he continued making his way through his guest lounge before starting to grab the belongings he'd take inside his place, once landed. Seeing the transfer case on the table, he decided to pick it up and have a gander at the 2.1 million unexpected bonus he'd secured. He entered the retrieval code and flipped open the carrier to see a digital readout that displayed: "0.000c." That wasn't right. Xavial was absolutely positive that the readout was "2,100,000c" when he took that case from Conoveh's cruiser. His stomach dropped, and he wracked his brain trying to figure out how that much money could have just vanished. It took all of four seconds before a single word popped into his head.

Vellakeen.

"Son of a..."

[—]

From the Author...

"Thank you for reading Disposable Dagger! I hope you enjoyed the story, and your support means the world to me. If you haven't already, please give Broken Hourglass a look as well. I look forward to being able to share more stories with you in the future!"

— Kielen King
kielen.king@monarkie.digital

About the Author

KIELEN (key-len) KING is a musician, author, and avid gamer. He is a lifelong science fiction fan, author of Broken Hourglass and Ion the Young Shuttle. Kielen continuously looks for ways to further the art of science fiction storytelling through various mediums.